HACKER

Leslie McGill

CAP CENTRAL

Fighter

Running Scared

Hacker

Copyright © 2014 by Saddleback Educational Publishing
All rights reserved. No part of this book may be reproduced in any form or by any means, electronic or mechanical, including photocopying, recording, scanning, or by any information storage and retrieval system, without the written permission of the publisher. SADDLEBACK EDUCATIONAL PUBLISHING and any associated logos are trademarks and/or registered trademarks of Saddleback Educational Publishing.

ISBN-13: 978-1-62250-707-8
ISBN-10: 1-62250-707-X
eBook: 978-1-61247-958-3

Printed in Guangzhou, China
NOR/1014/CA21401625

18 17 16 15 14   2 3 4 5 6

To the students and staff of Takoma Park Middle School.

CHAPTER 1

KESHAWN

"So how'd I do on my math test?"

Luther Ransome stopped his black Escalade in the middle of Seventeenth Street. A line of cars began to form behind him. His window was halfway down. He leaned across Chance Ruffin, who was sitting in the passenger seat. Although it was only seven in the morning, the bass booming on his radio was loud enough to rattle the window.

From where he stood on the sidewalk, Keshawn Connor could see Jair Nobles and Thomas Porter in the back seat. Jair, Thomas, and Chance were all moving in time to the beat of the music.

"Your real score? Fifty-nine percent," Keshawn said flatly. "Now recorded as a seventy-five. So your overall average is seventy something. You've got a C."

"My *man*!" Luther said, slapping his steering wheel. "I have an English test tomorrow. Make sure I pass it. I don't have time to study tonight."

As if you ever studied, Keshawn thought. *And why should he? He knows his grades will stay above passing. Even though he's never cracked a book.*

"Why are we talkin' to this loser?" he heard Thomas say from the back seat.

Keshawn turned back toward school. Luther rolled up the window, but then rolled it back down again. "Oh, and another thing," he said. "Make sure you take Neecy's seat in math today. I want her to sit by me."

Keshawn didn't bother to answer. No need. Luther knew Keshawn would do whatever he was told.

He was locked in a trap, and Luther held the only key.

CHAPTER 2

NEECY

Hey, Ferg! Whaddup?" Carlos Garcia called to his best friend, Lionel "Ferg" Ferguson.

Ferg turned and waited for Carlos to catch up. Together they walked down Seventeenth Street, turning at the corner of K Street toward the front door of Capital Central High School. The large high school was located in the northeast quadrant of Washington, D.C.

"Man, I am still feelin' that practice," Carlos said, making a face. "Coach seemed extra hard on us last night."

"True that," Ferg said. "He's still mad about that Cardozo game."

"I just want to forget that game!" teammate Charlie Ray said, walking toward them. "Down twenty-four at the half, and I couldn't hit a three to save my life." Charlie was tall, with short dark hair and eyes that were almost black.

"At least you made your free throws," Ferg said. "I shot like my sister does when we're playing horse."

"Hey, maybe Sierra should join the team." Carlos laughed. "I've played horse with her. She's not bad. And we may need a point guard."

"Isn't JaQuel the point guard?" Eva Morales asked, joining the guys.

Ferg threw his arm around Eva's shoulders and gave her a kiss. Ferg and Eva had been going out for over a year. They made a cute couple.

Both of them were a little overweight, but it didn't bother them. They were friendly and well-liked.

"He is for now," Charlie said as they opened the door to the school. "But he might not maintain eligibility. He needs a 2.0 GPA to play, but he has Ds in English and math. So Coach Williams gave him until the day report cards come out. If his grades aren't up by then, he's off the team."

"Man, that's cold," Eva said. "But everyone should know the rules. Bad grades should always get you tossed from the team."

"Yeah, it's harsh. Before Mrs. Hess came along, the rule was ignored," Ferg said. "I guess whenever there's a new principal, they make sure everyone follows all the rules. Since this is Mrs. Hess's first year, we're paying the price."

"This is the hardest year ever," Eva said bleakly. "I feel like all I do is study, and I still can't keep up."

"You guys talking about math?" Neecy Bethune, one of Cap Central's cheerleaders, joined them. She had her long straightened hair pulled back in a ponytail that swung when she walked. Her big brown eyes looked concerned.

"Yeah, math and English and US history and—" Ferg said, shaking his head.

"I hear ya," Charlie said. "All I do is practice and study. My game's off, and my grades are tanking. And baseball season is just around the corner. I *have* to make grades so I can play. If I can't play, I may as well kiss college good-bye. Getting a baseball scholarship is my last hope."

"Don't even talk to me about scholarships," Neecy said with a shudder. "I've kept my grades up every semester since middle school. I can't believe I might lose it this close to college."

"Oh, that's right! You're one of those D.C. Stars, aren't you?" Charlie said. "That seems so long ago."

"It was. That happened back in fifth grade," Neecy said.

"So what was the deal? Some rich guy offered to put you through college?" Eva asked.

"You make it sound like it was just me." Neecy laughed. "It was my whole fifth grade class. I lived over in Southeast at the time, and no one from that neighborhood ever went to college. So some guy said he'd pay for college to any kid in my fifth grade class who maintained a 3.0 GPA, as long as we stayed in D.C. public schools. Maybe he was hoping a lot of us would move out of the area. College costs a lot of money."

"So how many of you are left?" Charlie asked.

"Not many. Most didn't keep their grades up, and some moved out of D.C. The last time we got together, there were only six of us left. I'm barely hanging on—my GPA last marking period was barely a three. I can't believe I could lose the scholarship after hanging on for—what? Six years?"

"Now *that's* pressure," Carlos said, shaking his head. "But back to JaQuel. He *is* the team. He's that good. If he's ineligible, our season is over."

"Quel should get some help," Eva said. "I stayed after school yesterday with Mr. Sullivan to try to get caught up in math. It helped, I guess. I'm still lost, but not *as* lost."

"Right, miss practice for math help," Ferg said with a laugh. "Coach would have his ass if he tried that one."

"Sullivan's there at lunch too sometimes," Eva said as they wove through the crowds of kids talking and laughing in the hallway. "If JaQuel doesn't try to help himself, I don't feel too sorry for him."

"Get ready to feel sorry for the whole Cap Central basketball team if he doesn't make grades," Charlie said, looking dejected. "We need a miracle, and we need it soon."

"Well, he's still got a couple of weeks," Eva said. "So if he gets his grades up like the coach said, maybe you'll be all right."

"He'd better," Ferg said, shaking his head. "We play Wilson High School right after report cards come out. Those guys go to basketball camp all summer. I hear some of them have personal trainers. You know, helping them keep fit with strength training and stuff. If JaQuel can't play, we're screwed. No one else has his moves. And the D.C. tourney is right after that."

"Our season could be over almost before it gets started," Carlos said. "Man! I wasn't feeling so bad when I left home this morning, but now I'm totally miserable. Thanks, guys," he joked. The others laughed. "I'm gonna find Joss to cheer myself up," he added. "I'll see you later." He took off to find his girlfriend, Joss White, who was Eva's best friend.

"Ask her to show you her new glasses," Eva called after him. He waved without turning around.

"You want to stop at your locker before biology?" Ferg asked Eva.

"Yeah, I need to get rid of my backpack," she said. "See you guys later." She and Ferg walked off down the hall.

"You ready for Piper's class?" Charlie asked Neecy. They walked down the hall toward their first period English class.

Neecy nodded. "I stayed up late to finish *The Great Gatsby* last night," she said. "Are you done with it?"

"I finished it a day or two ago," Charlie said. "I thought it was pretty good."

"Me too," Neecy said. "And Piper is a relief compared to math. It helps that I had him in ninth grade before they switched him to teaching junior English. You know, it's too bad about Quel," she added as they stood outside their classroom. "It's gonna mess everyone up if he can't play."

"I think he knows that," Charlie said. "At least he tries to do his work. Some of those others, like Chance Ruffin, don't even care."

"Is he in danger of being ineligible too?" Neecy asked.

"I think lots of guys are," Charlie said. "Chance and Luther Ransome and—"

"Please. Do not even mention his name," Neecy said with a shiver. "I hate that guy."

"Really?" Charlie said curiously. "Why?"

"Lots of reasons," Neecy answered. "Among others, he's a cheater. Back in ninth grade, I saw him looking at my test in math. He wasn't even trying to hide it. All I do is study, and he tries to steal my answers. I don't think so."

The first bell rang, and they walked into Mr. Piper's classroom.

"You want to go to the library at lunch to work on math?" Charlie asked. "I can help if you want me to," he offered.

"Sure," Neecy said. "I'll see you there."

She looked up at the tall athlete and smiled. He grinned back at her and took his seat.

CHAPTER 3

KESHAWN

Keshawn divided his life into before and after.

Before was back when he didn't have a computer. When he heard other kids talking about games like *Halo* and *World of Warcraft,* and had no idea what they were talking about. Before he talked his mother into buying him a computer so he would do better on his schoolwork. Back when no one at Cap Central High School paid him any attention.

After could be traced to the day he helped his mother and grandmother install a computer program on that new computer. A program they'd heard about that would enable parents to monitor their children's Internet usage. A program that could be installed on any computer to capture passwords and access data.

Including the computers at school.

Later, when he remembered how it all started, he thought it was actually kind of funny. His mother and grandmother, two of the most technologically clueless women in D.C., got him started in his life of hacking.

The three of them lived together in his grandmother's house on Mount Olivet Road. The house was a wreck. There was no money to keep it up. His mother made next to nothing waiting tables at a lunch place in downtown D.C., and his grandmother was too sick to work. Keshawn often came home from school to find a note from the power company on the door saying that the service had been cut off. He wanted to help, but how could he? He didn't have a job.

The house was a short walk from All Souls Spiritual House of Love Eternal. Keshawn's mom and grandmother loved that place. They forced Keshawn to spend all day with them there on Sundays, surrounded by old ladies in big hats. The ladies who attended All Souls sprinkled quotes from the scriptures—or what they thought was scripture—throughout their conversations.

Keshawn knew his mother and grandmother hoped that dragging him to church for several hours a week would keep him out of trouble. "Train up a child in the way he should go, and when he is old, he will not depart from it," they warned whenever he tried to stay home.

It had the opposite effect. Sitting there for hours on Sunday afternoons gave him lots of time to think.

And to figure out ways to make some cash.

The plan wasn't yet on his mind when he first begged his mother to buy them a computer. He finally wore her down. She bought a basic model, signing a note to pay for it over a two-year period. Right after they got the computer, Deacon Sharpe at All Souls held a meeting where he invited a speaker to warn the congregation about the evils of the Internet. Keshawn's mother and grandmother came home and accused him of all sorts of things: looking at porn, chatting with strangers, gambling. Really? He was just playing games.

The speaker at the meeting conveniently had some spying software for sale. He convinced parents the software could be easily installed and used to capture their children's passwords and website visits. Which would have been helpful had anyone in the house besides Keshawn known how to use the software. His mom used a computer at work for placing orders and printing out her customers' checks, but she didn't even have e-mail.

And his grandmother? She sometimes tried to answer the phone by picking up the TV remote. Keshawn tried to teach her computer basics, but it was hopeless. So his mother and grandmother asked Keshawn to set it up for them. They quickly got lost trying to follow what he was doing. So they never saw that he chose the password that made the whole program work. The irony was that the only person in the family who could use the software designed to spy on Keshawn was Keshawn himself.

One day at church he was chuckling to himself about how funny it all was. Sometime between the second and third hour, as he started to doze off, he had a brainstorm. *Wouldn't it be cool*, he thought, *if I could read teachers' e-mails? Look at other kids' grades? Snoop around?*

Not to actually *do* anything—just look.

So he tried it. He copied the program onto a flash drive and brought it to school. He sat in the library for a few days and saw which teachers used which computers most often, like at lunch time. One very busy day, when the librarians were too busy to notice, he stuck his flash drive into one of the computers and installed the program. Then he logged off and sat at another computer. Soon Mr. Sullivan, his math teacher, came in and logged in. He did whatever teachers do, logged off, and left.

Keshawn moved to that computer and logged in. He opened the spy program, and there it was, Mr. Sullivan's user name and password plus all the sites he visited. Keshawn had access to it all, including the teacher's school e-mail and grade book for each of his classes.

Keshawn looked at his grades and those of others in the class. Charlie Ray, 84 percent. Rainie Burkette, 91 percent. The majority were in the 70-percent range. And then there were a few that were far, far lower. Including Cap Cent athletic superstar Luther Ransome. Quarterback, basketball player—name the sport, Luther played it, and played it better than almost anyone else.

But apparently his abilities stopped at the locker room door.

His average in math was 59 percent.

He had started the year okay but had flunked the last three tests. He also had lots of missed work. Keshawn looked around further and found a way to see overall grade point averages. Luther had the 2.0 GPA needed to be eligible to play sports—but just barely. That 59 percent, if it stuck, was going to pull his GPA down. Football season was just about over, and basketball season was about to begin. Report cards would be out in a couple of weeks. If his grades slipped, he wouldn't be able to play.

Unless he had some help.

Keshawn increased Luther's score on the last test to a seventy-five, added a few percentage points to quizzes, entered homework he hadn't turned in—did all sorts of illegal stuff to his record.

By the time he was done, Luther had an 86 percent. B-plus.

And a total, laughable lie.

Later, Keshawn couldn't even remember why he had done it. More than helping Luther

Ransome, it was just the thrill of being *able* to do it. He didn't even like Luther Ransome or his friends, and he couldn't pretend to care about Cap Cent sports.

Keshawn quickly tried to undo what he'd done. He lowered those that he remembered having changed. But of course he hadn't kept records and couldn't remember them all. Luckily, Mr. Sullivan returned all tests and other work after he entered the scores into the system. So there wouldn't be any record of Luther's grade except what was in the computer.

For some reason—pride maybe—Keshawn kept the score on that math test at seventy-five. He knew Luther wouldn't ever tell anyone if his grades miraculously got better. By the time he was done, Luther had a low C. Not his original grade, but high enough that he could play sports. Keshawn logged off and swore he'd never do it again.

And that should have been the end of it.

Except that it wasn't.

About a week later, Keshawn overheard Luther talking to Chance Ruffin, a friend of his. For some reason, Luther always let Chance hang around. Maybe because they were teammates. Chance also played both football and basketball. But where Luther had street smarts, Chance was a thug. Stupid, big, and mean. Likely to be in jail or dead by the time he was nineteen.

Anyway, Keshawn heard Luther tell Chance that he was worried he wasn't going to be able to play basketball because his grades were so bad. He said something to the effect of, "I'd pay anything to get my grades up."

That got Keshawn thinking.

Luther had the money and the bad grades. Keshawn had the computer access and needed the cash.

As the church ladies would say, a match made in heaven.

Keshawn waited until a day when lots of Cap Cent kids were hanging out on the hill behind the school. On a clear day, you could look out over Washington, D.C., and see the Washington Monument way off in the distance.

Keshawn hung around, waiting for Luther. When he saw him come out the school's Maryland Avenue door, he stepped in his path. And he made him an offer.

Money for grades.

What happened next was the most humiliating thing that had ever happened to Keshawn.

Luther laughed at him. Just threw back his head and howled.

"Homes, I am *not* about to pay you to tutor me," he said when he caught his breath. "Luther Ransome does *not* need to be schooled!"

Keshawn later realized this was one of many signs that he should have walked away. He had always hated people who referred to themselves in the third person.

But if he was honest, he knew why he didn't leave. His pride was hurt. Here Keshawn was offering Luther an illegal, sophisticated way to solve his problem. Instead of being impressed or grateful, he ridiculed Keshawn for what he thought was an offer of tutoring.

Tell him what he can do to himself and walk away, Keshawn's conscience and dignity advised.

Tell him how much he needs you, his wounded ego urged.

Ego won.

Keshawn told him he had found a way of

changing grades. That he would change any grade for twenty bucks each. He even told him the first change was "on the house," so he could see that Keshawn could actually deliver.

"Your fifty-two percent on that math test last week?" Keshawn said, all cocky. "If you're interested, say the word and it will go from failing to a C."

Keshawn stood a little taller when he saw Luther's look of respect.

"For real? You can do this?" he asked.

Keshawn nodded.

"But how?" he asked. "Is there any chance we'll get caught?"

"None," Keshawn said confidently.

What a joke. Keshawn had no idea if he could get caught doing this or not. But he didn't want to show Luther any weakness.

Even Luther was perplexed at Keshawn's motives.

"Why are you doing this?" Luther asked.

"I don't know," Keshawn said. He didn't want to say it was for the money. Then something made him add, "You seemed like you could use a friend."

A look passed over Luther's face that Keshawn couldn't read. He tried to convince himself that it was gratitude. It wouldn't take long for him to learn that it was the way Luther showed total contempt.

"Well, thanks," he said. "But I'm not convinced you can make this work. So go ahead, do it," he said. "And if you're successful, I'll start paying you."

"It's done," Keshawn boasted. "Check your grades online. That fifty-two doesn't exist."

Luther looked at Keshawn long and hard. "My man," he said finally. "I think we can do a lot of business together."

His fist bump made Keshawn's heart soar. He hoped the whole school had seen it. Luther Ransome didn't act friendly like that to just anyone. Especially a nobody geek. Keshawn figured his coolness stock had just gone up.

By then, Luther's friends had seen that he had arrived on the hill. "Hey, dawg, let's eat," Thomas Porter said.

Thomas Porter had transferred to Cap Cent a few weeks into the semester. He was a bad dude. Just the kind of guy Deacon Sharpe warned parents about.

Luther started to walk away. "I'll catch up with you later," he said to Keshawn.

Keshawn nodded and went to the library.

He was so proud to have a skill that a guy like Luther Ransome needed. It felt really, really good.

As the church ladies would say, pride goeth before destruction, and a haughty spirit before a fall.

CHAPTER 4

NEECY

Eva walked down the long corridor and made it into Mr. Sullivan's second period math class a minute before the late bell rang. She started for her usual seat beside Joss White. Before she could sit down, Keshawn Connor pushed a few desks out of the way and sat down quickly in the desk behind Eva's. That desk was beside Rainie Burkette, who was already working on the day's warm-up exercise.

Rainie looked up in surprise. Keshawn sat where Neecy usually sat. Eva shot a questioning look at Joss and Rainie. Both girls shook their heads in confusion. Eva put her backpack under her desk and turned around.

"Keshawn?" she said.

"What?" he asked.

"You know you're in Neecy's seat," Eva said. Mr. Sullivan didn't actually assign seats, but the girls had been sitting together since the first day of school.

"What difference does it make?"

"Makes a difference to us," Eva said.

"That's been Neecy's seat since September, and she'll want to sit there," added Rainie.

Keshawn didn't move. For a moment, it looked as if he was going to make a big deal over it. But instead, he gathered up his books and stood up.

"Seriously, Keshawn," Rainie said.

"Whatever," he said. He picked up his backpack and walked to the front.

"Thanks," Eva called out to his back. But he didn't turn around. "What the heck was that about?" Eva asked Joss and Rainie as she sat down.

"I have no clue," Joss said. "That was so random. Where does he usually sit?"

"He usually sits way in the back," Rainie said.

"Really?" Joss said. "I've never paid attention to him. But sitting with us is just weird."

"Probably thinks you're hot, like every other guy in the school," Eva said.

"Oh, puh-leeze!" Joss laughed.

"What did Carlos say about the glasses?"

"He said I look smart," Joss said. "That's only because he knows I'd kill him if he said they made me look like a geek."

"You couldn't look geeky if you tried," Eva said.

"Luther, leave me *alone*!" Even in the middle of the room, the girls could hear Neecy's voice from the hallway. She burst through the classroom door and whirled around. She looked tiny against the huge football player standing behind her.

"I am really tired of you messing with me," she said angrily. "And why are you always laughing at me, Chance?" she said to Chance Ruffin, Luther Ransome's best friend. "You need to leave me alone. It's not funny anymore."

"Girl, you say that to me now, but like I told you, it ain't over with Luther Ransome till Luther Ransome says it's over," Luther said with a sneer.

"Over? It never started," Neecy hissed. She

walked to her desk and sat down. Her anger made her face flush.

Eva and Joss turned in their seats to face Neecy. "What was *that* all about?" Eva asked.

"Ugh. Give me a minute to calm down," Neecy said. "Okay, here's the story. A couple of weeks ago, I was walking home from school and Luther caught up with me. He said he 'just happened' to be walking in my direction. I should have realized something was up because he lives over by Gallaudet University. And he never walks anywhere. He drives that big Escalade. Anyway, he walked as far as my house with me. When we got there, he asked me if we could hook up sometime."

"Ew. He actually said 'hook up'?" Eva asked with a disgusted look. "Just like that?"

"I know, right?" Neecy said. "He's got no class. But anyway, I was so shocked by his question that I didn't answer the way I should have. I should have said that I wouldn't hook up with him if he were the last guy on the planet. Like, if the choice was for me to hook up with Luther or all of mankind would be doomed, I'd kiss mankind good-bye."

The girls laughed.

"So you didn't tell him that you were willing to sacrifice the whole human race rather than hook up with him," Joss said. "How *did* you answer him?"

"I sort of hemmed and hawed. I honestly was so stunned by his question that I don't even know what I answered. But I guess I wasn't as clear as I should have been because he's been annoying me ever since. He calls and asks when we're gonna hook up. He's always texting me at night. And lately he's been following me. Either him or Chance Ruffin. And *he's* just plain creepy. At least Luther doesn't scare me the way Chance does."

Mr. Sullivan walked into class right as the bell rang. "All right, class, let's get started," he said.

"Luther and Chance both give me the jimjams," Eva whispered. "Nothing I can ever put my finger on. But I just don't trust either one of them."

"Me neither," Joss said. "Look at them now."

Luther Ransome was talking angrily to Keshawn Connor. Keshawn had taken a seat in the front of the room. Luther was gesturing over his shoulder toward where the girls were sitting. Keshawn looked down at his desk with a miserable expression. Chance looked at the girls and wiggled his tongue in and out before he and Luther took a seat.

"Oh, yuck," Eva said.

"Does he think that will make us want him or something?" asked Rainie.

Joss laughed so hard she snorted.

Neecy looked away. "Please. I don't want him to think I'm even looking at him," she said. "But wait, I'm not done. Last night, I texted Luther back and told him I was never going to hook up with him, and I wanted him to leave me alone."

"What did he say?" Joss asked.

"He said no," Neecy said. "No! Who says no to that? And what do I do now?"

"Ladies," Mr. Sullivan said firmly. "Considering some of your grades in this class, I would advise you to pay attention."

The class got quiet as they worked on the warm-up exercise displayed on the whiteboard.

Neecy completed the first two steps of the problem but then got stumped. She looked around the room. It seemed like everyone else was getting it.

Mr. Sullivan looked up from his desk and saw Neecy looking around. "Miss Bethune, approach please," he said in his formal manner.

Neecy put down her pencil and walked to the front of the class.

"You're in real danger of failing this class," he said in a low voice. "You seem to be falling further and further behind. I've never seen you at my after-school homework club where I could help you get caught up. Do you just not care?"

"I do care, Mr. Sullivan," Neecy said. "In fact, I probably care more than anyone in this room. I'm one of the D.C. Stars."

"So that means you have to maintain a 3.0 GPA to qualify for the scholarship, right?" Mr. Sullivan asked.

Neecy nodded. "I know I'm struggling in this class, but I'm really trying, I promise," she said. "I'm just not getting it. Is it possible to move to an easier math class?"

"I'm not ready to recommend that," Mr. Sullivan said. "But I suggest you come for extra help before grades are released. Because once the grade has been recorded, it's on your permanent record. That's what the D.C. Stars people will see. Let me check where you are now." He hit some keys on his computer keyboard. "Hmm. Not good. Not good at all," he said. "You have a sixty-eight average. Unless you get it up, and soon, that will be recorded as a D."

"I know. I'll try harder," Neecy said. She turned and walked toward her seat. Luther Ransome turned sideways in his chair and stuck out his leg, blocking her path.

"Really?" Neecy said. She kicked his leg out of the way and went back to her desk.

The door to the room opened and JaQuel Rivas walked in.

"Nice of you to join us," Mr. Sullivan said sarcastically.

"Sorry," JaQuel said, sitting in the empty desk near Neecy.

"Please get to work on the warm-up," Mr. Sullivan said.

"Neecy, do you have any idea what's going on in this class?" JaQuel whispered.

"None," Neecy said.

"This class is killing me," JaQuel said. "And I have to pass it. If I don't make grades, I'll get kicked off the basketball team. Already the guys are starting to give me grief about that. As if I'm doing it on purpose!"

"JaQuel, Neecy, please stop talking and get to work," Mr. Sullivan said.

"Mr. Sullivan, it's hopeless," Neecy said. "I am so lost."

"All right, who wants to explain it to Neecy?" Mr. Sullivan asked. "Anyone?"

The class was quiet. Finally, Rainie Burkette raised her hand. "I can try," she said.

Rainie had always been one of Cap Central's top students. She had a part-time job, and lately she'd started running a lot. Neecy wondered how she was able to keep up her grades with all her extra activities.

"Come up here and play teacher for a minute," Mr. Sullivan said. "Since you're the only brave one in the class."

Rainie stood in front of the whiteboard and bit her lip. She then began writing numbers and symbols while explaining what she was doing.

When she got to the end, she turned to Mr. Sullivan with a sheepish smile. "I'm falling down at the end here," she said.

"You did fine," Mr. Sullivan said. "But you got a little off track right about there." He pointed to one set of numbers. "Neecy? How about it? Can you see where Rainie made her mistake?"

Neecy laughed. "Not a chance, Mr. Sullivan," she said.

"I can do it," Charlie Ray said.

He stood up and walked to the whiteboard. Erasing some of Rainie's figures, he quickly finished the problem.

"Thank you, Doctor Ray," Mr. Sullivan said playfully. "Some of you who are struggling should get on Charlie's good side so he can help you over the hurdle. Now let's get to work on today's lesson."

He walked up to the whiteboard and began to teach.

Luther Ransome turned in his seat and looked back at Neecy. He pointed to her and then pointed to himself. Then he nodded slowly.

"I hate him," Neecy whispered.

CHAPTER 5

KESHAWN

Keshawn felt like such an idiot. He really liked that group of girls: Eva, Joss, Rainie, and Neecy. Their crowd was friendly. They must have thought he was crazy taking Neecy's seat. But Luther told him to do it.

He had no choice.

He had to do whatever Luther told him to.

As the church ladies would say, lie down with dogs, wake up with fleas.

Or as Keshawn Connor told himself fifty times a day, *you have only your own stupid self to blame.*

He could have pulled the plug on the whole rotten scheme before he had gotten in any deeper. But he didn't. And by the time he realized the trap he was in, it was too late to escape.

After Keshawn had made his offer, Luther didn't say anything for a few days. Keshawn had checked Luther's grades online and saw that his changes had not been corrected. Apparently, the alterations were not discovered.

About a week later, Luther stopped Keshawn as he left school one afternoon. He asked him to come sit in his car for a minute.

His car was beautiful—on the outside. A big black Cadillac Escalade. Keshawn climbed in and was shocked at the condition inside. It was trashed. Taco Bell and McDonald's wrappers, empty soda cans, and lots of athletic clothes thrown everywhere.

Later, Keshawn realized the car was just like Luther. Looking good on the outside, but a mess on the inside.

To quote the church ladies, pretty is as pretty does.

"I just want to make sure I understand what you're offering," Luther said. "I think I was so surprised that you actually wanted to help me that I didn't pay real close attention last week. Tell me again."

"Sure," Keshawn said. Even to himself, he

sounded too eager. "I have access to the database. I'm not going to tell you how."

Who do you think you are, James Bond? a little voice inside Keshawn's head warned. After all, he had only tried this one time, with one teacher's grades.

"So I can tweak your grades anytime you need me to," he continued. "All you have to do is pay me twenty bucks a pop, tell me what grades you want changed, and I'll do it."

"But isn't this illegal?" Luther asked.

Right, Luther Ransome, the Boy Scout. When Keshawn looked back on this conversation, he couldn't believe he didn't see what was coming.

"Of course it is." Keshawn laughed in what he hoped was a manly, conspiratorial tone. "But that's what you're paying me for."

"I don't know," Luther said. "It seems dangerous. And wrong." He put his hand in his pocket.

"Don't worry about it," Keshawn said. "I know what I'm doing. I came to you, not the other way around."

"Okay, fix Chance's math grade so he's passing," he said.

Keshawn had never offered to do anyone else's grades, only Luther's. So he shook his head no. "Sorry, dude," he said, trying to sound slick. "Too risky to make too many changes."

"You'll do it, *dude*, and you'll do it for free," Luther said, his voice dripping with contempt. "Along with anything else I tell you to do. And here's why."

He pulled out his cell phone and touched the screen a few times. Keshawn's voice came out loud and clear:

Keshawn: I have access to the database. I'm not going to tell you how. So I can tweak your grades anytime you need me to. All you have to do is pay me twenty bucks a pop, tell me what grades you want changed, and I'll do it.

Luther: But isn't this illegal?

Keshawn: Of course it is. But that's what you're paying me for.

Luther: I don't know. It seems dangerous. And wrong.

That's it, Keshawn thought. *My life is officially down the toilet.*

Luther could play that recording to anyone, and they'd know that Keshawn was responsible. In fact, it sounded like Luther was declining Keshawn's offer. If the school ever accused Luther of somehow changing his own grades, he could easily say that Keshawn had made the offer. And Luther could be heard saying it was wrong.

Keshawn was screwed. Luther could now blackmail him into doing pretty much anything he asked. The grades were already changed, so there was proof that Keshawn had hacked into the school's network.

Unless, Keshawn thought with a start, *unless there was no proof of what the original grades had been.*

"And I still have all my returned tests and assignments," Luther said, as if he had read Keshawn's mind. "So I've got all the evidence I need."

He turned the key and the big car's engine roared. "So change Chance's math grade. And get out of my car. You're stinking it up."

Some people wait their whole life to screw up, Keshawn thought to himself. *Me? I managed to do it in eleventh grade.*

CHAPTER 6

NEECY

Neecy ate a quick lunch and went to the library to meet Charlie. Most of the computer desks were taken. She walked to her favorite spot, the quiet desk in the back of the room. Too late, she realized that Luther Ransome was already sitting there. She turned quickly, but not before he saw her.

"You want to sit here?" he asked innocently. "No problem. I'm just about done."

Neecy walked back toward him, planning to wait till he logged off. But instead, he put his arms around her waist and pulled her down onto his lap. "You can sit right here!" he said. He held her so tightly she couldn't pull away.

"Let me go," she hissed at him, scrambling

to get loose. But all he did was laugh and hold her tighter.

"Let me go!" she said in a louder voice. She was aware that other students were peering around their computers to see what was happening.

"Here you are," Charlie Ray said, walking back to where Neecy sat on Luther's lap. "I saved you a computer up in the front so I could show you that work you missed."

He held out his hand, and she took it.

With all eyes on him, Luther released his grip. The look he flashed Charlie was filled with hate. Neecy stood and walked with Charlie to another bank of computers.

After logging on, she turned to Charlie. "Thanks, Charlie," she whispered. "You saved me from that creep."

"He's a piece of work," Charlie said. "Thinks he's the next Michael Jordan, Cam Newton, and the rest of the sports world all wrapped up in one package."

"He thinks he's God's gift to women too," Neecy said. "But most girls I know can't stand him. The ones who do like him are pretty skanky."

"I'll bet he's not too happy with me right

now," Charlie said with a laugh. It was clear he wasn't worried about it. Charlie was popular with everyone: athletes, science team members, even the drama club. No one could ever be angry with Charlie.

"Well, you're my hero," Neecy said. Her computer booted up. She entered her user name and password and went to the D.C. school system's website where grades were posted. "Oh, Charlie, I wish I was half as smart as you are," she said. Her grades were so low, there was no way she was going to maintain a 3.0 when report cards came out.

"What makes you think I'm so smart?" Charlie asked with an amused smile.

"Are you kidding? Everyone knows you're a genius!" Neecy said with a laugh.

"Actually, everyone just *thinks* I'm a genius," Charlie said. "I'm pretty average."

"You are not!" she said hotly. "Ask anyone. Ask the teachers. They always call on you."

"If I tell you a little secret," Charlie said, "can you promise not to tell anyone?"

Neecy nodded, wondering what he was about to say.

"I'm not as smart as people think I am," Charlie said. "Not even close to it."

"Oh, I don't believe you!" she said with a laugh. "Your definition of smart and my definition of smart just aren't the same."

"I get decent enough grades," Charlie said. "But seriously? I'm just okay. Except at baseball. I'm pretty spectacular at baseball."

"Hmm," Neecy said. "I always figured you were smart. I didn't know you were athletic too."

Charlie snickered, startling the students working on the surrounding computers. The librarian shushed him.

"I'm more than athletic," he bragged, flexing an arm muscle.

Neecy put her hands over her face to stifle her laughter.

"I will probably get a baseball scholarship because I am that good. I have an arm that Superman would like to have. This is not bragging; it's the truth. But I'm *not* particularly smart."

"Modest much, Charlie? Which arm?" Neecy said.

"Which arm what?" Charlie responded.

"Which is the arm that Superman would envy?"

"The one you're sitting beside," Charlie said. "Might be worth a couple million someday," he added. "So watch it!"

"So I shouldn't do this?" Neecy said, punching him softly.

"What was *that*?" Charlie asked.

"A punch." Neecy laughed.

"Yeah, a *girl* punch," Charlie said. "I don't think I'll need rehab."

Right then, Mr. Piper, their English teacher, sat down in the seat on Neecy's other side. He spread out folders, grade books, and other materials and turned on the computer.

Neecy turned back to her screen and accessed her assignments webpage. Out of the corner of her eye, she was distracted by Mr. Piper shuffling materials around. He had spread his folders and books out in the space between the two computers. "Sorry, Neecy," he said pleasantly when he saw her looking at the mess. "I'm sort of a slob."

He turned on the computer and started hitting keys. Neecy tried concentrating on her computer screen, but he was getting agitated. Finally she looked over at him. His log-in screen was still up with nothing in the password window.

"Something wrong?" she asked.

"I can't remember my new password," he said. "They make us change them about every two months. And we can't just use a new number after the same word, like 'sparky1,' 'sparky2,' and so on. So I can never remember mine. I have it written down here somewhere, but I don't know where."

Neecy looked at the disordered mess of papers overlapping her own work. "What did you have it written on?" she asked.

"A yellow sticky note," he said. "So if you find it …"

Neecy nodded. "Sure," she said. "You could just change it."

"I've already changed it about three times in the past month," he said. "I wish they'd just let me keep the same one. I'm not real tech smart. Am I, Charlie?" he asked, leaning past Neecy to where Charlie Ray was sitting. "Charlie knows. He's helped me with this stuff before."

“Nothing like a smart tech support guy, right, Mr. Piper?” Neecy said innocently.

Beside her, Charlie laughed.

“I know, right?” Mr. Piper answered. “Now if he could just tell me my darn password or where I left it.”

“Were you working on any other computers before this?” Charlie asked. “Teacher’s lounge? Your classroom?”

“Yes to both,” Mr. Piper said. “So maybe I left it at one of those computers.” He moved too quickly and a pile of papers slid onto the floor. Neecy bent down and helped him pick everything up.

“I’m a total mess,” Mr. Piper said. “And I don’t feel like going back upstairs to find that sticky. Wish I could remember what password I’m using this week.”

“Your dog’s name? Your birthday? Your phone number?” Charlie said.

“Oh, right,” Mr. Piper said, turning back to his screen. He typed in a few letters and the computer came to life. “How’d you know?” Mr. Piper asked with an incredulous shake of his head.

"Just smart, I guess. Those are the passwords everyone uses," Charlie whispered to Neecy. "And that's why people around here think I'm so smart. I'm really just logical."

Neecy covered her mouth to keep from laughing out loud.

"Hello, Neecy, Charlie. Hey, Ed." Mr. Sullivan walked behind them a few minutes before lunch was over and took an empty seat beside Mr. Piper. "Must be lots of things due around here. These are the only computers free in the building." He logged in to his computer and plugged in his flash drive.

"Neecy, I hope you're working on your math," Mr. Sullivan said. "There's not much time between now and when report cards come out. It's not impossible for you to get your math grade up before then, but you're going to have to work hard."

"I'm actually helping her with her math right now," Charlie said. Neecy bit back a smile. Since sitting down beside Charlie, she hadn't done any work at all. But she was grateful that Charlie made it look like she was willing to work.

"That so, Neecy?" Mr. Sullivan asked. She nodded. "Well, he's got his work cut out for him. Nothing you can do about your grades so far, of course," he added. "But maybe you can pull yourself out of the hole you're in with the next couple of assignments and the unit test. "

Neecy looked at the time on her computer screen. The bell indicating the end of lunch was about to ring. No time to get any work done today. Even though it was against the rules, she quickly accessed her e-mail account. No mail. She logged off and gathered up her materials.

"I saw that," Charlie said with a chuckle.

"Well, don't tell on me," Neecy said.

"I don't know. You broke the rules," Charlie said. "I may have to e-mail someone about this."

Neecy looked at his computer screen and saw that he too had accessed his e-mail.

"Busted!" Neecy said with a laugh. "Oh, wait, I forgot. Smart kids never get in trouble here, do they?"

"Oh, yeah?" Charlie said, shaking his head.

Neecy stood up to leave. She did a double take when she saw Luther Ransome leaning against the wall near the bank of computers. She hadn't seen him standing there. His face radiated pure hatred. She looked to see who he was looking at.

He was staring at Charlie Ray.

The bell rang and students shut down their computers. Keshawn Connor stood up from the computer across from Mr. Piper. He picked up his books and started for the door of the library.

As Neecy watched, Luther Ransome grabbed Keshawn's shoulder roughly. The larger boy bent down to say something, then motioned with his chin in Neecy's direction. Keshawn nodded and turned back toward the computers.

Neecy wondered what Luther had said. She simply could not imagine anything that Luther Ransome and Keshawn Connor would have in common to talk about. She also couldn't imagine anything Luther might have said that would cause Keshawn to return to a computer in the library.

Keshawn was a nice guy. He blended into the rest of the Cap Central crowd, never standing out in any particular way. He was always friendly. He was nothing like Luther Ransome or his posse of thugs.

He was certainly not one of the usual Luther Ransome wannabes.

The whole thing was very mysterious.

CHAPTER 7

KESHAWN

Keshawn watched the whole Charlie Ray–Luther Ransome drama with dread. He knew Charlie had just made an enemy of the most evil person at Cap Central.

Luther was already in a foul mood. He was furious that Keshawn hadn't stayed in Neecy's seat in math, the way he'd told him to. Keshawn had tried to explain, but of course it didn't help. At one point, Luther even pulled out his cell phone.

As if Keshawn needed to be reminded of the recording Luther had made.

When the bell rang, Keshawn tried to escape from the library without Luther seeing him. But no such luck.

"Get their passwords," he said, gesturing toward Neecy and Charlie.

By now Keshawn had installed the keystroke-tracking program on all the library computers. That part wasn't difficult. He was actually amazed that the school didn't have some sort of protective barriers in place to prevent people from installing programs.

He had captured a few teachers' log-in information. It was slow going. The computers were so well used that he had to get to them as soon as a teacher logged off, or there was too much data to wade through.

He sat down at the computers and quickly captured Charlie's and then Neecy's user names and passwords.

"Keshawn, you're going to be late for class," the librarian called.

"I'm leaving," he said, pulling out his flash drive.

As he pushed in his chair, he saw a yellow post-it note on the floor.

Mr. Piper's user name and password.

One more teacher whose records he could access. He didn't even have to use his spyware for this one.

CHAPTER 8

NEECY

After cheerleading practice, Neecy went home and turned on her computer. She had lots of homework, but first she checked her e-mail.

She saw that she had messages from Eva, Joss, and other friends. But the message that was most intriguing was from someone named GoodTimeCharlieRay.

She opened it.

I really liked talking 2 u 2day. I have liked u 4ever. I know this sounds crazy, but I am 2 shy to talk 2 u about this. If you're ok with this, give me a sign in school tomorrow? But don't mention this e-mail, ever. I don't do stuff like this, and I feel awkward. Charlie

Neecy read the e-mail several times. It was odd. It didn't sound at all like Charlie. He seemed more confident in real life than he came across in the e-mail. For most people it was the reverse.

She had always liked him, but did she *like* him? The thought made her smile.

The e-mail was very mysterious. She wasn't supposed to mention the e-mail—just give him some sort of sign in school. She started thinking about what sort of sign she could give him. She finally decided what she would do. It would leave no doubt as to how she felt about his e-mail. As she fell asleep, she had a funny thought: she never even considered saying no.

The next morning, Neecy hopped out of bed before her alarm. She took special care to make sure she looked good. She got to school early and stood around the K Street entrance, waiting for Charlie.

Soon students started arriving. By seven fifteen, the front courtyard was full of kids. Neecy stood on her tiptoes, straining to find him. In the distance, she saw Carlos Garcia and Ferg Ferguson walking up Seventeenth Street toward the school. She watched as Joss White and Eva Morales caught up with them. The two couples walked toward the school, but soon they stopped. All four students turned around. Neecy could see Charlie Ray walking behind them. He joined the others, and soon they got close to where Neecy was standing.

"Hey, Neecy, great sweater!" Eva said as they approached.

"Thanks," Neecy said, distracted. She looked at Charlie, searching for some indication that he liked her as much as his e-mail had indicated. His expression was as friendly as usual. He didn't look questioning or awkward or conspiratorial. Neecy had to appreciate the effort it must have taken him to have kept his expression neutral.

"How did you do on that math homework?" Charlie asked.

Neecy wondered if that was some sort of obscure reference to having sent her an e-mail while she was doing her homework.

"It was … interesting," she said. "I struggled with the meaning for a while, but then I figured it out."

"*Interesting?*" Charlie repeated with a laugh.

"I don't know that that's the word I would have used. But then, I don't ever find math assignments all that interesting."

As*sign*ments! That was it: a very secret reference to his e-mailed request for a sign that she liked him.

Neecy started to smile, then broke out in a big grin. She stood on her tiptoes, put her hands on either side of his face, and kissed him full on the lips.

"I like you too, Charlie," she whispered.

Then she turned and walked into school. As the front doors started to shut behind her, she turned around. Joss, Eva, Carlos, and Ferg were frozen in place. They all stared at her with stunned looks on their faces.

But Charlie? Charlie looked like he'd been hit by a truck. His jaw had dropped, and he didn't even notice that he'd dropped his backpack.

"Bye, bye!" She waved and walked off to class.

CHAPTER 9

KESHAWN

Keshawn laughed to himself when he saw Neecy kiss Charlie.

Because this one was on him.

Luther hadn't told him to actually do anything with Neecy's and Charlie's e-mails—yet. But Keshawn watched them in the library, and he could see they were starting to like each other. When he saw the murderous look in Luther's eyes, he decided to speed up the process.

Keshawn needed to feel good about something. The situation with Luther made him feel like a total screw-up. In his heart, he knew he was a better person than that. So he decided to use his technical power for good to try to balance out the bad.

He used his keystroke-tracking program to

capture Neecy's and Charlie's e-mail account names, passwords, and log-in information. That night, he set up a fake e-mail account and called it "GoodTimeCharlieRay." He figured there was no chance in the world that Charlie would have ever used such a cheesy name.

Keshawn sent the e-mail from that account to Neecy, asking for "the sign" and telling her not to mention it. He then went into her e-mail account and deleted the e-mail. He also deleted the fake account.

It worked beautifully. Neecy planted a juicy one on Charlie. Keshawn figured they could take it from there.

He would have enjoyed knowing how they figured out the GoodTimeCharlieRay e-mail that started the whole thing, but he wasn't going to read his friends' e-mails. Although he had no qualms about reading the e-mail of someone who was not a friend.

Like Luther Ransome.

He'd been reading Luther's e-mail for a couple of weeks now. His account name was "HandsomeRansome." His password was NFL2B.

Yeah, right, Keshawn thought when he first saw it. *DCJail2B is more like it.*

He looked around Luther's e-mail without leaving any trace. He wanted to be prepared. He knew it might come in handy some day.

Those church ladies' voices were echoing in his head again. I run on the road long before I dance under the lights.

Keshawn just *knew* that one wasn't from the scriptures. He looked it up. It was from Mohammed Ali.

CHAPTER 10

NEECY

With only a short time left in the marking period, many Cap Cent students were panicking. Mr. Sullivan's after-school homework club was crowded, as more students came in for help. Neecy came every day. JaQuel Rivas came, as well as Charlie Ray and Durand Butler. Even Rainie Burkette, one of the smartest students in the school, started coming in for help.

"I am swamped this semester," Rainie said to Neecy as they headed upstairs to Mr. Sullivan's class. "I feel like I don't even have a moment to myself."

"I hear you," Neecy said. "I'm exhausted, but so stressed that I can't even fall asleep anymore."

"I'll be really glad when Mr. Sullivan's test is over next week," Rainie said. "I'm even running numbers in my head when I'm running. It's all I'm thinking about!"

The girls went into Mr. Sullivan's class. Mr. Sullivan was helping Eva Morales at the whiteboard.

The door burst open and a large, noisy group of guys came in. Luther Ransome was there, along with Chance Ruffin, Jair Nobles, Thomas Porter, and a few others.

"Hey, Sully," Luther said, looking around the room.

"Luther, gentlemen, please come in. I'm glad you've decided to try to get caught up."

Luther started to laugh in an insulting tone. "Oh, I'm not here for help, Sully, my man," he said. "I'm looking for Keshawn Conner. Seen him?"

"Not today, Luther. But if you're not here to work, I suggest you and your friends get out of my room so that these students who do care about their grades can continue."

"I think Sully's disrespecting me!" Luther said, turning to Chance Ruffin. Something about his posture changed, and he looked a little intimidating.

Chance walked behind Mr. Sullivan's desk. He picked up a paperweight and a picture frame and set them down again.

"Chance, get out from behind my desk," Mr. Sullivan said. "I'm not disrespecting any of you. I am giving you a choice. Take a seat and work on math … or leave."

In the back of the room, Charlie Ray tapped Durand Butler on the shoulder. Durand was a wrestler and his muscles showed it.

"Think he needs help?" Charlie asked.

"Let's just wait," Durand said. The two boys watched Luther carefully.

As if he knew they were watching him, Luther looked their way. When he saw Charlie, his face changed from a smirk to raw hatred.

"I'm watching you, Ray," he said nastily.

He stood still for a moment, and then turned suddenly. "Let's get away from these losers," he said. He and his friends slammed the door loudly as they left.

For a moment no one spoke.

"Well, that was interesting," Mr. Sullivan said. "Now, where were we?"

CHAPTER 11

KESHAWN

The whole school seemed to know that Luther was looking for Keshawn. There was a time when Keshawn would have enjoyed the attention. But now he couldn't even remember why he ever thought it would improve his prestige. The more tangled up Keshawn got in Luther Ransome's drama, the more he realized how few people even liked the guy.

He could hear the church ladies now: live and learn.

Keshawn found a quiet spot far away from the trophy case in the main lobby of the school. He wanted to get some work done. But mostly, he wanted to hide from Luther. His plan didn't work. Keshawn heard some loud voices. He peered around the corner and saw Luther and his posse coming down the hall. His heart sank. Luther looked even more angry than usual. He knew Luther was going to give him a new set of instructions.

Luther put out a hand to stop his boys from going any farther.

"Who do you think you are, Connor?" he asked. "I need to talk to you. And when I need to talk to you, I need to find you. Fast. So I don't waste my time looking. Now get over here."

Keshawn slowly got up and crossed to the side of the hallway. He didn't want the others to overhear what Luther was about to say.

"Did you change Chance's grades yet?"

"I don't have access to all his teachers' passwords," Keshawn lied. "They don't all use the library computers."

"Well, get in there and do it," Luther snapped. "The team doesn't have time to wait to find out if he's gonna play guard. And make him get a good grade on Sullivan's math test next week."

"Yes, sir," Keshawn said sarcastically.

"And mine too, obviously," he said.

"Obviously," Keshawn echoed.

"And take this," he said, handing him a flash drive. "There's a picture on it. I want you to install it on Sullivan's computer account."

"What is it?" Keshawn asked.

"Let's just call it insurance," Luther said with a nasty laugh. "In case he tries to get cute. Oh, you can look at it if you like," he added. "Might get you hot."

This guy is sick, Keshawn thought. *I just want out.*

Now.

"Look, Luther, can't we just quit this now?" Keshawn asked. He knew it was futile, but he was so tired of the whole thing. "I'll change your grade and Chance's. But can't we stop at that point?"

Luther pulled out his phone and rubbed the side. "Do I have to remind you?" he said.

Keshawn knew Luther was referring to the taped conversation. It seemed like a year ago when he'd first made him that stupid offer.

"No," he said miserably.

I have to end this, Keshawn thought. *I need to find a way to make it go away.*

Without getting expelled.

CHAPTER 12

NEECY

In the week before Mr. Sullivan's math test, Neecy checked with Charlie every night after doing her math homework. After they went over her answers, they would talk—sometimes late into the night.

The night before the test, Neecy went online to check her grades. The only way she could maintain a 3.0 was if she got a C or higher in math. And the only way she could get a C in math was if she scored at least a 75 percent on the test. Any lower and she would get a D in the class.

"I'm not sure I can do it," she told Charlie. She had already said good-night to her mother and was talking on her cell phone from bed. Without ever really talking about it, Charlie and Neecy had become a couple.

"I have total confidence in you," he said. "You work really hard. That's worth something."

"You're very sweet," Neecy said. "But it's math, remember? You're either right or wrong."

Charlie was quiet for a moment. "Can I ask you something?" he said finally.

"Of course," she said.

"Why—crap, this is really hard," he began. "Why did you kiss me that day?"

"What?" Neecy exclaimed. "You know *exactly* why! You asked me for a sign."

"A sign?" Charlie said. "What kind of sign?"

"Charlie Ray, quit messing with me," Neecy said. "Don't try to play innocent."

"Neecy, I'm sorry, but I have no idea what you're talking about," Charlie said.

"The e-mail you sent me. Saying you liked me, but that I needed to give you a sign that I liked you too. Remember?" Neecy said.

Charlie was quiet for a moment. "Neecy, before you kissed me, I never sent you any e-mails," he said. "The first time I e-mailed you was a day or two *after* you kissed me."

"Okay, now stop it," Neecy said. "You really think I'd just plant one on you out of nowhere?"

"Well, no," Charlie said. "I mean, look at me. How could you resist, right?" he joked. "But seriously. I didn't e-mail you. Do you still have the e-mail?"

"No, and that's sort of strange," Neecy said. "I went back to look at it, because when you e-mailed me a few days later, you used a different e-mail address. So I was curious about your first one. But when I went to retrieve it, I couldn't find it."

"What was the address?" Charlie asked. "How did you know it was from me?"

"It was from GoodTimeCharlieRay, I think at Gmail."

"Seriously? Like in 'Good Time Charlie'? Please tell me you didn't really think that's the account name I would use."

"Well, who else could it have been from?" Neecy said. "Of course I thought it was from you!"

"Tell me again what it said?" Charlie asked.

"I don't remember the exact words. Basically that you liked me but were too shy to do anything about it. So I needed to give you a sign as to whether I liked you too."

"That's crazy," Charlie said. "It doesn't even sound like me. I mean, I'm glad this all happened, and remembering that kiss keeps me warm at night. But I have to tell you, I didn't write that e-mail."

"Then who did?" Neecy asked. "And why? And whoever did it had my actual e-mail address. How?"

"No clue," Charlie answered. "But however it happened, I'm glad it did. I don't know if I would have made a move on you if you hadn't kissed me."

"So if you didn't send the e-mail," Neecy said thoughtfully, "you must have been a bit surprised."

"Surprised?" Charlie said with a laugh. "Surprised doesn't even come close. Stunned is more like it."

"Now I'm embarrassed," Neecy said. "I really thought you liked me."

"Did like you. Do like you," Charlie said. "Somebody did us a solid."

"Neecy! Get off the phone and go to bed," Mrs. Bethune yelled from down the hall.

"I gotta go," Neecy said. "See you tomorrow."

"Neecy? I hope we find out who wrote that e-mail," he said. "So I can thank them. Now get some sleep."

The next morning Neecy ran into Mr. Sullivan in the hall.

"I hope you're feeling okay about this test," he said. "I know you've been working hard."

"I hope I do okay," Neecy said. "I feel better about it than I used to, but I have to get a seventy-five on the test to get a C in the class, and I don't know if I can do that."

"Well, do your best," Mr. Sullivan said. "You might be surprised. There are actually some people doing better in this class than I had thought. I looked over everyone's averages last night. There were quite a few surprises."

"Hey, Sully, let's get the party started." Luther Ransome held up his hand to fist bump Mr. Sullivan. When Mr. Sullivan went to bump his fist back, Luther pulled his hand away and laughed meanly. He walked into class and sat down. Mr. Sullivan shook his head in disgust.

"Lots of surprises," Mr. Sullivan said softly.

The test was hard. Neecy felt like she got

some of it but ended up getting lost toward the end of some problems. She wasn't at all sure she had scored a seventy-five.

Two days later she learned the bad news when Mr. Sullivan passed back the tests. Not enough to get a C for the class at 72 percent.

That night, she checked her final grade online. Just as she thought, her average in the class had slipped. Unless a miracle happened between now and three days from now when report cards came out, her GPA would sink below 3.0. She was in serious danger of losing any chance for the D.C. Stars scholarship.

She broke the news to her mother. Neecy had to look away when she saw the tears in her mother's eyes.

"Is there anything you can do?" her mother asked. "Is it over?"

"There's always next semester," Neecy said. "This means I'll have to get mostly As to bring my average up."

"What about talking to your teachers?" her mother asked. "I think you should do anything you can to squeeze out a few more points. You're so close. It would be a crime to throw away this opportunity."

"I didn't throw it away," Neecy said. "Mom, I've kept my grades up every year since fifth grade. I'm one of maybe six D.C. Stars left. This semester is just so hard."

"Well, maybe if you did schoolwork instead of hanging out with your friends and talking on your phone so much," her mother shot back. "I've heard you talking late into the night this week," she added. "I've never heard you talk so much."

" 'Cause I've been getting help on my math," Neecy shouted. "Charlie Ray, one of the smartest guys in the school, has been tutoring me. I just can't do it. I'm not smart enough to go to college."

"You're more than smart enough," her mother said. "And you'll figure something out. You'll have to. Without that scholarship, your chances for college are gone."

"Don't you think I know that?" Neecy cried. "I'm doing my best."

"Well, you must do better than that," her mother said. "Whatever it takes to keep your scholarship? That's what you have to do."

Her mom walked out of Neecy's room and slammed the door. Neecy threw herself on her bed and buried her face in her pillow.

CHAPTER 13

KESHAWN

Keshawn knew he had to find some way to get out of the mess he'd created. But if he quit changing the grades, Luther Ransome could turn him in. Luther would play the tape, and Keshawn would be out of school before the day was out.

He sat in church one Sunday afternoon thinking about what he had done. He knew Deacon Sharpe would tell him to turn himself in. He believed in honesty, no matter the consequences. Keshawn's mother and grandmother did as well. What he had been doing was completely outside the reality of these good people. He wished he could talk to someone about it. Gotten some advice about how to get out of the mess. But there was no one.

He got himself into it, and he had to get

himself out. Hopefully without getting caught. Because the consequences of what he'd been doing would be dire. For sure he'd be expelled. From Capital Central and maybe from all D.C. schools. And he wasn't sure, but he suspected that what he had done might even be against the law.

That would be ironic, Keshawn thought. *I'll be the smartest computer geek in jail.*

He couldn't just quit changing grades. But he needed to find a way to quit being *able* to change the grades. And the only way he would no longer be able to change grades would be if his access to the database were blocked. The only way that would happen was if the school figured out what was happening. Once they knew they'd been hacked, Mrs. Hess and the rest of the school administration would scramble to fix the holes in their sloppy security. Then no student—no matter how skilled—would have access to the database ever again.

As the church service entered its third hour, he started to work on a plan. For the plan to work, he had to choose just the right moment to put it into play. It had to be after grades were posted online—but before report cards were actually printed. It would take some military-style precision.

As the church ladies would say, timing is everything.

He also needed to find the right person to use as his unwitting accomplice. Someone who he could count on to be totally honest. Someone with too much integrity to put up with dishonesty.

In other words, someone *not* like him.

Keshawn thought long and hard about who to use. He needed someone who the school administrators would never believe had tampered with the grades.

Luther Ransome was obviously out. As was anyone who hung around with him.

And other athletes were out as well. Each of them was under too much pressure to remain eligible to play. Keshawn couldn't trust that any of them would do the right thing.

But one name kept popping into Keshawn's head.

Neecy Bethune.

He had no way of being certain that she

would do the right thing. But he had to give it a shot.

"Hallelujah!" he yelled.

The church ladies all turned and looked at him, startled.

"It is good to express joy in church," Deacon Sharpe said from the pulpit. "Let us all say it together: Hallelujah!"

CHAPTER 14

NEECY

Report card day.

Mr. Sullivan told the class to break up into small groups to work on some problems. Neecy and Rainie moved their desks to form a group with Joss, Eva, and JaQuel.

"I am getting so pumped for the game against Banneker this weekend," Eva said. "Do you think we have a chance?" she asked JaQuel.

"Depends on whether we can all play," he said. "And that depends on what our report cards say this afternoon."

"Hey, why the long faces?" Luther Ransome asked, sitting in an empty desk. He moved the desk so that it was right beside Neecy.

No one said anything to him. Finally, he

laughed. "I'll bet you're all worried about your grades, right?"

"Pretty much," Neecy said.

"Not me," he said. "Luther Ransome doesn't worry about grades. And I already checked. I'm good to go," he added. "How 'bout you, Quel?"

"I don't know," JaQuel said. "It's close. I hope I'm over the line."

"You're lucky you only need a 2.0 to be eligible," Neecy said. "I think I may have dipped below 3.0 this semester."

"No way!" Joss said. "Are you sure?"

"Yeah, unfortunately. I checked last night."

"Well, maybe you'll be surprised," Joss said sympathetically.

"Neecy? Is your group ready to present the answer to the first problem?" Mr. Sullivan asked.

"Uh, not quite," Neecy said.

"Some other group?" Mr. Sullivan asked the class. Another group volunteered. Neecy tried to follow what they had done, but she was too lost.

Finally, the bell rang. As she packed up her books, Mr. Sullivan said, "Neecy? Could I see you please?"

Neecy stopped at Mr. Sullivan's desk. Charlie stood at the door and waited for her.

"I hope you're not going to be too surprised when you see your grade in this class," he said. "I know you have a lot riding on maintaining your grades. Hopefully, your average across all your classes will permit you to keep your scholarship. As always, if you want some extra help, I'm here."

"Thanks, Mr. Sullivan," Neecy said.

"So I guess it's official. I got a D," she said to Charlie.

"You know, he didn't actually say that," Charlie said. "I was listening very carefully to what he said. He said he hoped you wouldn't be too surprised when you saw your grade. That could mean anything."

"I love that you're so optimistic," Neecy said. "I guess I'll know soon."

The last class of the day was cut short so that students could go to homeroom to get their report cards. Neecy reluctantly looked over the paper, knowing what she'd see.

But she gasped in surprise.

Instead of the D she had expected in math, she had a C. Her heart soared. The C was enough to bring her average up to above a 3.0.

She didn't know how Mr. Sullivan had justified giving her that grade. After all, she had seen her grades posted online and knew exactly what her average in the class was. The school's computer calculated the grade based on the data inputted by the teachers. So he had to have changed something. She was curious about where he had made the change.

Whatever it was, it was enough to put her in the safety zone.

When she got home that afternoon, she logged in to the online grade system to check her grades. What she saw took her breath away.

Instead of the 72 percent she'd gotten on the last test, Mr. Sullivan had posted a 99 percent.

Neecy felt sick.

She needed the C, but she didn't want to get it this way. This was a lie. She didn't deserve that C, and she knew it. And she knew that Mr. Sullivan knew it as well. It made her lose respect for him. Grades were supposed to mean something—you worked hard and you got good grades. You didn't work hard, or you couldn't understand the subject, and you got bad grades. But not working hard and getting the same grade you would have gotten by doing a lot of work? That wasn't right.

Later, she called Charlie as soon as she knew he was home from basketball practice. She told him what Mr. Sullivan had done. She also told him how conflicted it made her feel.

"Do you want to talk to him?" Charlie asked.

"I'm not sure it would do any good," Neecy answered. "Now I realize what he was telling me today. He changed my grade. I had thought he was warning me that my grade would be bad. But like you said, he never really said that. He just told me I might be surprised."

"So what do you want to do?" Charlie said. "He really put you in a bad spot. He shouldn't have done it, but he was trying to help you."

"It doesn't sound like him, though," Neecy said. "It makes me see him in a whole other way. I don't respect him for doing this. I could always count on him to be fair in the past. This isn't fair."

"Well, whatever you decide, I've got your back," Charlie said. "I'll talk to you later."

Neecy could barely concentrate on her homework. She was too distracted by the dilemma she faced.

She worked hard in her others classes. She got the grades she deserved. Thank goodness those grades were good enough to maintain her GPA. But math? There was no way she deserved that C. She knew it. Mr. Sullivan knew it too. It seemed so unlike him to do something so wrong.

Neecy stared out of her window, wondering what to do. In the distance she saw a Metro bus pull up to the corner. Her mother got off. She looked tired, as she often did, making her way to their apartment from her job as a secretary for the federal government.

Neecy knew that her mother was desperate for Neecy to receive the D.C. Stars scholarship. In fact, her mother was more anxious about it than Neecy was. The last thing she wanted to do was tell her mother about the math grade. She was afraid her mother would want her to keep her mouth shut. And she knew how much that would destroy her respect for her mother.

She heard the front door open. She could

hear her mother's slow footsteps coming up the stairs.

"Neecy? You home?" her mother called out.

"In here," Neecy said, not getting up.

"So? How'd you do?" her mother asked.

Silently, Neecy handed over the report card. She watched as her mother searched for the grade point average.

"Yes," her mother yelled, pumping a fist in the air. "You did it! I have to say, I was a little worried. I mean, not worried, exactly. But it just didn't seem like you were studying as much. If you don't get this scholarship, I mean—I know you'll get it, you're a good girl, a smart girl—"

"Mom, *stop*," Neecy said loudly. "Just stop it!"

"Well, I'm sorry, but I was just so worried. You know this report card is so important—"

"Mom, this report card is a lie. My math grade isn't right."

Neecy's mother was quiet for a moment. "Well, maybe you did better than you thought?" she said.

"No, I know exactly what grade I deserved," Neecy said dejectedly. "And it wasn't a B. The grade is too high."

"Too ... too high?" her mother asked.

"Too high," Neecy repeated. "There is no way I have a C in math. I got a D. I saw it online the day before grades were posted. Something's wrong, and I don't know what to do about it."

Her mother was quiet for a moment. "So if the grade is wrong and it gets corrected ..." she said.

Neecy could see her mother's shoulders sag as the knowledge sunk in of what a lower grade would do to her average. They looked at each other silently for a moment.

"What are you going to do?" her mother asked finally.

"I want to keep the grade," Neecy said. "But it doesn't seem right," she added in a whisper.

Neecy's mother was silent.

"Oh, Mom, I know I'm letting you down," Neecy said, tears coming to her eyes. "But this is wrong."

"Do you think I'm going to be disappointed in you for telling the truth?" her mother asked. "Really?"

"What do *you* want me to do?" Neecy asked.

"You know what? I'm not going to tell you

what to do," her mother answered. "I'll just lay out the facts. You got a grade you didn't deserve. I don't know how that happened or why. I just know what you're telling me: your math grade is not correct. So you have two choices. You can keep silent, get your scholarship, and know—for the rest of your life—that your success was built on a lie."

Neecy sat on the edge of her bed and put her face in her hands.

"Or you can tell someone at the school that a mistake has been made and get the grade corrected. There's a high price for each choice. On the one hand, the cost of getting the grade changed is huge—four years of college costs. Money that you won't get for college otherwise. On the other hand, you have to think about the cost to your conscience. But in the end it's your choice. Either way, you're losing something. It's just a question of what's most important."

"Mom, I'm so sorry," Neecy said. "I blew this scholarship thing. And it was such a gift."

"It *was* a gift," her mother agreed. "I'm not sure it's totally blown, since you still have another marking period to get your grades up.

But it's up to you. Either way, you have to live with your decision for the rest of your life."

Neecy covered her face with her hands. "So you won't tell me what I should do?" she asked miserably.

"If I told you, it would be my decision, not yours. And you could blame me for the rest of your life," her mother said. "This is far too serious to have someone else decide for you. I'm sorry, but this is what real life is. Stuff happens, and there's no one but you to handle it. Sounds cold, but that's life. I'm going to go take off my shoes and make us some dinner."

Neecy didn't look up as her mother left the room. She was more confused than ever.

CHAPTER 15

KESHAWN

As the church ladies would say, desperate times call for desperate measures.

Keshawn changed Chance's and Luther's grades. Geniuses. Both of them. If Mr. Sullivan ever looked back at this semester's grades, he'd know right away that his account had been hacked. But there was no way to guarantee that he'd look at grades for a semester that was already over.

So Keshawn also changed Neecy's grade.

He knew all about the D.C. Stars. He'd heard her talking. He knew how important it was to her to keep her grades up. By changing the one grade that put her back to a 3.0, Keshawn knew he had put her in a terrible jam. But her stress about her scholarship made her extra careful, so he knew she would know it wasn't just a casual error.

Knowing Neecy, he was sure she must be agonizing over what to do. He was sorry for that. But it had to be done.

But that's not all he did.

He didn't want the school to take the easy road and just tell Mr. Sullivan to change his password. He needed the school to delete the keystroke-tracking program from the computers. He also needed to make sure the school system plugged its sloppy security. No more installing tracking programs.

He accessed Mr. Piper's grade book and changed the grades of kids he didn't particularly like. Gave them all As. Then he did the same thing in Dr. Miller's biology class. He figured it would be harder to identify who had done it if the students who benefitted weren't his friends.

He only hoped that Mr. Sullivan would report the hacking immediately. For his plan to work, Mrs. Hess needed to tell the rest of the teachers to check their grades too. The school would then see how widespread the dishonesty was. Then maybe they'd tighten up their computer security to keep this from ever happening again.

As those big-hat-wearing church ladies would say, locking the barn door after the horse gets out.

The next day Keshawn ran into Luther before school. Luther motioned with his head toward the courtyard in the center of school.

They walked outside.

"Did you put that picture in Sullivan's computer like I told you?" Luther asked.

"Yep, buried where only I can find it," Keshawn lied.

Buried was right. He had taken a hammer to the flash drive, then threw it in a trash can along Bladensburg Road. But he did save one copy of the picture, just in case.

"You need to send it to me in an e-mail. I need it to look like it's from him to me. Think you can handle it?"

"I'm in people's e-mail all the time," Keshawn boasted. "I think I can handle it fine."

Figure it out, NFL2B, Keshawn thought. *That means you*. "What do you want the e-mail to say?" he asked.

"Something like, 'I'd like to do this to you.' Something pervy like that," Luther said. "My e-mail address is HandsomeRansome. I need it to be in my list of received mail in case I ever need to say he was messing with me. Clear?"

"Crystal," Keshawn said.

Luther wasn't satisfied ruining only Keshawn's life. Now he was trying to ruin Mr. Sullivan's life as well.

"Oh, and I want you to send an e-mail from Neecy to Charlie Ray. Tell him that she wants to break up with him, and that she doesn't want to talk about it. Be really cruel, so he's too hurt to talk to her."

He wants to ruin my life, Mr. Sullivan's life, and now Neecy and Charlie's lives as well, Keshawn thought. *He is out of control*.

He had to find a way to disable Luther Ransome.

Not physically, though he had to admit, he wouldn't cry if Luther got hit by a Metro bus.

No, Keshawn needed to find a way to make

sure that Luther never tried to use that recording against him. He had to find a way to blackmail Luther so Luther could no longer blackmail him.

Right now, Luther could use his recording to make sure Keshawn did what he was told. He had to come up with something just as powerful to use against Luther. They'd both have a threat they could use against the other. Not a pleasant way to live the rest of their lives in high school, but necessary.

He just had to think of something.

CHAPTER 16

NEECY

Neecy barely slept. She weighed her options and neither felt right. If she told Mr. Sullivan that she wanted him to change her grade back, she might be throwing away tens of thousands of dollars in scholarship money. In fact, it might mean she couldn't go to college at all.

But if she didn't say anything, she knew that for the rest of her life she would know that what she had achieved had been based on a lie.

The choice was impossible.

She was angry that Mr. Sullivan had put her in this position. He should have given her the grade she deserved. Teachers should do the right thing. It shouldn't be her responsibility to tell him to be honest.

She finally gave up trying to go back to sleep. She got dressed and left early for school.

As she walked up Seventeenth Street, she ran into Carlos and Ferg. "Hey, did you hear our good news?" Ferg said when she caught up to them. "The whole basketball team made grades!"

The two boys high-fived each other.

"Even Luther and Chance?" Neecy asked. "They never work in math class."

"I don't know," Carlos said. "I just know that we all had to show our report cards to Coach Williams yesterday. It's all good."

Neecy shook her head. There was no way that Luther or Chance could have passed math. She knew how hard she'd studied for the final test, and she only got a seventy-two. Luther and Chance often ditched class, and rarely turned in any homework.

That settled it. She was disgusted that Mr. Sullivan would change grades for students who didn't deserve it.

Charlie joined the group and put his arm around her. "So what did you decide?" he asked softly so the others couldn't hear.

"I'm talking to him," Neecy said firmly. "I hadn't decided until just this minute. I want good grades, but not this way. It makes me no better than those creeps."

"You know, if you ask him to change your grade back, he may feel he needs to change theirs back too," Charlie warned. "Not that I'm telling you not to do it."

"That's their problem," Neecy said angrily. "I'm not going along with something wrong just so the school can win basketball games."

"You going to wait till class?" Charlie asked.

"No, I'm going to go see him now," Neecy said. "If I talk to him in class, everyone will know."

"Well, good luck," Charlie said. "And for the record? I think you're doing the right thing."

Neecy gave him a half smile and took the front stairway up to the second floor. She stood in the doorway of Mr. Sullivan's room. She needed a moment to get her courage up. Accusing a teacher of dishonesty was not easy.

"Neecy, good morning," Mr. Sullivan said pleasantly. "What can I do for you?"

"Mr. Sullivan, I need to talk to you about

my grade," Neecy said. She hated that her voice came out all squeaky.

"I think you got the grade you deserved," Mr. Sullivan said gently. "I'm sorry that it was a surprise to you."

"But that's just it," Neecy said. "It was a surprise because it was wrong. I didn't deserve that grade. I track my grades online. I knew what to expect. You shouldn't have changed my test grade. It's a lie."

Mr. Sullivan looked confused. "Neecy, I'm afraid I have no idea what you're talking about," he said finally. "Are you saying you think you should have gotten a better grade on the final test?"

"No," Neecy said. "I mean, yes, I should have, because I should have done better. But I got a seventy-two on the test, and you posted it online. Then when I looked again, it changed to a ninety-nine! I appreciate that you were trying to help me keep my D.C. Stars scholarship, but it's not right."

"A ninety-nine?" Mr. Sullivan said incredulously. "*Ninety-nine?*" he repeated. "Neecy, in sixteen years, I can probably count on one hand the number of students who scored that high on my tests. I didn't change your grade once I recorded what your test score was. Maybe you saw something else? A homework assignment?"

"It was the test," Neecy said. "I've probably checked it fifty times. It brought my grade way up, which would have been great. But it's a lie."

Mr. Sullivan hit some keys on his computer. "Let's take a look," he said. "Okay, here's your class. And you have a—What?! You're right. A ninety-nine on the test," he said. "What did you say you actually got on the test?"

Neecy pulled the graded exam out of her backpack. "Seventy-two," she said.

"I can't imagine how I made that mistake," Mr. Sullivan said. "Did you say you had seen the seventy-two earlier?"

"I did," Neecy said. "I saw it the day you returned the tests. Then when I got my report card, I was so surprised by my grade. I checked online to see how I could have gotten a C in your class. That's when I found the ninety-nine."

"But I didn't post any grades after I recorded the test scores," Mr. Sullivan said slowly. "So for it to have changed ..."

All of a sudden, his expression darkened. His eyes narrowed and a hard look came over his face.

"Are you kidding me?" he hissed, staring at the screen.

"Excuse me?" Neecy asked.

"Neecy, yours isn't the only grade that's been changed," he said disgustedly. "This is very serious, and I need to get to the bottom of it. It may take me a while to figure out what's going on. In the meantime, you should keep this conversation to yourself. I don't want your name involved. What's going on needs to be reported to Principal Hess."

Neecy said she'd keep quiet and then turned to leave.

"Neecy?" Mr. Sullivan said.

She stopped and turned back.

"It took a lot of courage to do what you did," he said. "And I know you could really use that C. So I'm really, really proud of you for telling me about the error."

"It wouldn't have felt right to keep quiet," Neecy said sadly.

She turned and walked out of the room, practically bumping into Luther Ransome.

"Hey, Neecy, whatcha doing in Mr. Sullivan's room all by yourself so early in the morning?" Luther asked with an evil leer. "Getting a little extra attention?"

"Leave me alone," Neecy said. "You're disgusting."

"That's not what you said last night," he said loudly. Several students looked at them in surprise.

"Actually, that's what every girl who's ever gone out with you has said," Neecy shot back.

Luther threw back his head and laughed. "Babe, I'm sorry I didn't take you up on it when you asked me to hook up with you. But you really got to get over it! Though looks like Mr. Sullivan's helping you forget about me."

"You're trippin'," Neecy said. She turned in the other direction and walked away.

CHAPTER 17

KESHAWN

As he walked to class, Keshawn saw Neecy coming out of Mr. Sullivan's room. As soon as he saw her, he knew she was telling the teacher about her altered grade. Keshawn knew he had made the right choice when he chose her as his unwitting accomplice. For the first time in a long time, he felt a little optimistic.

Particularly since he had spent the evening putting part two of his plan into action.

He had set up a fake e-mail account using the name "TeacherCrusher." It meant nothing, but Keshawn figured Luther would think it had a dirty meaning. Then he sent an e-mail from that account to Luther.

Keshawn worded the message carefully. He wanted Luther to think it was inappropriate, and everyone else to think it was innocent. So he wrote a message that could go either way.

When I saw this picture, I got excited. I really want to see you do this.

He attached a picture to the e-mail, but first he changed the file format so that Luther couldn't open it easily. A computer tech could fix it in a flash. But he hoped Luther wouldn't have the skill or patience to try. After all, Luther thought he knew what it was.

Which brought Keshawn to part three of the plan. It would be much, much harder to execute. He would have to choose his moment carefully. It would also require him to forfeit any chance of ever looking cool.

He hoped he had the courage to actually do it.

CHAPTER 18

NEECY

Hey, guess what?" Charlie said on the phone that night. "Coach told Luther and Chance they couldn't practice today because there's something weird going on with their grades."

"Weird? How?" Neecy asked.

"I don't know. I just know they weren't allowed to practice. Something about their grades in math and biology."

"Both? That's interesting," Neecy said. "I wonder if their English grades were wrong too. My English grade was correct."

"Remember that day when they came in? We were working with Mr. Sullivan, and Chance got behind his desk. Do you think he did something to his computer?"

"It's possible," Charlie said. "It will be

interesting to see what happens tomorrow. Now, how's that homework? I gotta tell you, I have no idea how to do number eight."

They worked on homework for a while and then said good-night. As Neecy got ready to go to bed, there was a knock on her door.

"Neecy? Can I come in?" her mother asked.

"Come in, Mom," Neecy replied.

"I just wondered what you decided to do," she said as she sat on the end of Neecy's bed.

"I told Mr. Sullivan I didn't want that fake grade," Neecy said. "Sorry, Mom, if you're disappointed. But I wouldn't have been able to live with myself if I had kept it."

"Baby, I am so proud of you," her mother said. "You did the right thing. The honorable thing. No matter what happens in your life, you can always look yourself in the eye and say, 'I did the right thing.' Not everyone can say that."

She hugged Neecy close. "And, hey," her mother added. "Isn't it about time I met that young man of yours?"

Neecy laughed. "I'll tell him," she said. "Good night, Mom. And thanks."

"For?" her mother said.

"I guess for leaving it up to me, but believing in me too."

"You make me proud to be your mom. Now get some sleep."

The next day, Neecy and Charlie went to the cafeteria at lunch. Soon Eva, Joss, Ferg, and Carlos joined them. More students came and sat down.

"I am so pumped for the game this week," Carlos said.

"I actually think we have a chance at winning," Durand Butler said. "Hopefully Luther and Chance will get their report cards straightened out and can play. But at least JaQuel can be our point guard."

"I am still so amazed that Luther and Chance made grades," Rainie Burkette said. "I think Mr. Sullivan's class is impossible. And *I* keep up with the work."

"I know, right?" Eva said. "At least JaQuel worked hard. He was in there almost every day getting extra help. But Chance? I don't understand how he passed. Or Luther for that matter."

Joss looked across the cafeteria to where

Luther and his friends were sitting. Luther and Jair had earbuds on, in violation of the school's rules. Luther's cell phone was laying on the table in plain sight—also against the rules.

"I can't stand those guys," Joss said. "They think the rules don't apply to them."

"Hey, what's Keshawn doing over there?" Ferg asked. "I can't see him as part of Luther's posse."

The students all watched as Keshawn Connor started walking toward Luther's table holding his lunch. As he got closer, Luther said something to his friends. They all laughed meanly.

Keshawn didn't seem to notice. He stopped by Luther's chair and leaned down to say something to him. As he did, he popped the top on his soda can. With a whoosh, soda shot out all over Luther, Chance, and the others at the table.

Luther and Chance jumped up swearing. Everyone at the table tried to move things out of the way. Keshawn lost his grip on the can, and it bounced onto the table. The sticky liquid kept spraying everything in its path.

Keshawn dove for the can, but that just

made things worse. It was total chaos. Finally, Keshawn put up his hands and began backing off. Even from across the room, Neecy's group could hear him say, "Sorry! Oh man, I am so sorry. I can't believe I did that."

He looked totally embarrassed as he left through the cafeteria doors. It wasn't until a few seconds later that Luther let out a roar.

"Where is my phone?" he shouted.

CHAPTER 19

KESHAWN

The whole cafeteria saw Keshawn spray an entire can of soda on Luther and his friends.

They thought they'd all witnessed the most embarrassing moment of Keshawn's life.

No one knew that it was staged. A distraction to cover up Keshawn's true intent. There was so much confusion, it took Luther forever to realize that his phone was gone. Keshawn had slipped it into a pocket of his cargo pants.

He didn't want to be caught with the phone on him. So he went to the restroom on the first floor. He used a paper clip to open a paper towel dispenser. He stuck the phone way in the back and locked it up again. He planned to retrieve it when it was safe. He was going to take a hammer to it, same as he did with the flash drive. Then toss it in a trash can far from school, where it was destined to become landfill.

The door opened and a group of guys came in. They were all Luther's friends, and they weren't happy. They washed the sticky soda off their arms, and a few used paper towels to blot their jeans.

"You're a moron, you know that?" Chance Ruffin said.

"Hey, sorry. Really!" Keshawn said. "It was an accident."

It wasn't, but they'd never know that.

"I oughta pound you for this," Thomas Porter said.

Great, Keshawn thought. *Just the guy I want to have mad at me.*

"This crap is all over me," Jair Nobles said, rubbing his jeans with a paper towel. "I can't sit through class like this. What's wrong with you?"

Before Keshawn could answer, the door opened and Mr. Gable, the school security guard, came in. "We're not going to have any trouble in here, are we, gentlemen?" he asked.

No one answered.

"Get to class," he added, holding open the

door. Chance went through first, then Keshawn slipped out. The others followed. If security looked at the tapes from the camera outside the restroom, Keshawn didn't want it to look like he came and left by himself. It would look suspicious.

That afternoon, the school office called Keshawn's classroom to tell him to come down to the office. Mrs. Dominguez, the office secretary, asked him to go into the principal's office.

"I understand there was some trouble at lunch," Principal Hess said.

"I spilled a drink," Keshawn said innocently. "I felt bad that it got so many people wet."

"Some of the people involved said that it looked like you might have done it on purpose," she said.

Keshawn tried to look outraged. "On purpose? Why would I do that?" he asked. "I was totally humiliated."

"Hmm," Mrs. Hess said thoughtfully. "Any idea what happened to Luther's phone?"

"No. Did he lose it?" Keshawn asked.

"Apparently in the chaos after you spilled your drink, he lost it somehow."

"Sorry I can't help," he said. "I was soaked after my drink spilled, so I went right to the restroom to clean up." He knew the security camera would back this up.

"Security is searching lockers while I'm speaking to everyone involved. Anything you'd like to tell me before they go to your locker?"

"Uh … I've been planning to throw out those old sneakers for a while?" he said with a grin. "No, nothing, Mrs. Hess. They're welcome to look."

"And you probably won't mind pulling out your pockets for me," she said.

Keshawn wasn't sure she was allowed to ask that, but he wasn't going to go all legal on her. He pulled his own phone out of his pocket and put it on her desk.

"That one's mine," he said. Then he pulled his pockets inside out. "Okay?" he asked.

"Yes," she answered. "I appreciate your cooperation. Now you can go back to class."

He left her office looking somber. But as soon as he got to where he knew he was out of range of the school cameras, he pumped his fist in the air.

CHAPTER 20

NEECY

The next day, Mrs. Dominguez called into Neecy's first period class and asked that she come down to the principal's office.

As Neecy walked down the stairs, she ran into Luther Ransome and Chance Ruffin.

"What's going on, girl?" Luther asked.

"No clue," Neecy answered truthfully.

"Do you know, homes?" he asked Chance.

"Dunno nothin'," Chance answered.

They waited in the outer office for a few minutes. Mrs. Dominguez got a call and then stood up.

"You may go in now," she said. "You're in the conference room."

Neecy led the way into the large room across from Mrs. Hess's office. At the door, she stopped so suddenly that Luther walked into her. Sitting around the table were Principal Hess, Mr. Gable, Mr. Sullivan, Mr. Fisher—the district's tech support guy—and a couple of other men in suits. There were two laptops open on the table.

"Come in, Neecy. Hello, Luther and Chance. Please come in and take a seat," Mrs. Hess said.

Neecy sat in the first open seat. She didn't know what this was about, but she didn't like the feel of it.

"Students, the reason you're here is because we've found some irregularities in your grades," Mrs. Hess said.

Neecy looked at Mr. Sullivan. He was looking at Luther, as if to watch for a reaction. Mr. Sullivan seemed to sense Neecy looking at him because his eyes shifted her way. As their eyes met, he winked. Neecy realized it was his way of telling her not to worry. She relaxed a bit.

"What kind of regularities?" Chance said.

"*Ir*regularities," Mrs. Hess corrected. "Grades have been changed. We're here today to find out how it was done."

Luther had said nothing so far. His arms

were crossed in front of his chest. Neecy noticed that he was wearing a Washington Redskins football jersey with the number twenty-one. The same number he wore on Cap Central's football and basketball teams.

"I know my grade was changed, but I have no idea how," Neecy said. "I told Mr. Sullivan when I realized it. I think it was changed the day after our final test."

"How did you discover the change?" one of the men in suits asked.

"I checked my grade online after Mr. Sullivan gave us back our exams, and I had gotten a seventy-two," Neecy explained. "Then I got my report card, and my math grade was much higher than I expected. I checked again and my exam grade was a ninety-nine."

Beside her, she felt Luther jerk, as if he'd gotten a cramp.

"Luther, you look like you'd like to say something," Mrs. Hess said.

"Nah, I'm cool," he said. His voice sounded funny, like his jaw was stuck.

"Your grade was changed as well," Mrs. Hess said. "Had you noticed?"

"I don't bother to check my grades much." Luther smirked. "I'm not obsessed with school like Neecy."

"That's interesting, because your online account shows you logged in the day after Mr. Sullivan said he returned the tests. At eight thirty at night," Mr. Fisher said, looking at the laptop.

"Any explanation, Luther?" Mrs. Hess asked.

"Okay, look, you're right," he admitted. "I knew my grade had changed. But I just figured Mr. Sullivan changed it for some reason."

Mr. Sullivan gave a short laugh.

"How about you, Chance? Did you notice any changes to your grades?"

"I never check my grades," Chance said gruffly. "And I didn't even get that test back. I wasn't in class that day. So I wouldn't know if the grade I got was right or not."

Mr. Fisher hit some keys. "There's no sign that Chance accessed his school account. In fact, it looks like he never even set it up with a user name or password."

"Did either of you change your grades?" Mrs. Hess asked.

Luther and Chance both yelled at once.

"No way!"

"Get out of here!"

"Okay, okay, calm down," Mrs. Hess said, holding up her hand. "Do either of you have a suspicion as to who changed them?"

"Besides Mr. Sullivan?" Luther asked.

"Right," Mrs. Hess said. "Any other ideas?"

No one said anything. Had Luther been smarter, Neecy would have bet that he had done it himself. But she knew he didn't have the skill to circumvent the school's computer security.

But she knew he somehow played a role. She just knew it.

"Let me just say something here," Mrs. Hess said. "This is a serious security breach. Whoever did this is in big trouble. Whoever comes clean first is going to be looked at favorably by all these people. Those two are from the school system's security team. And this gentleman is a D.C. police detective assigned to the public schools."

Neecy knew she hadn't done anything wrong. And yet, she was terrified. She felt like she was going to go to jail. She couldn't imagine how she would have felt had she actually done this herself.

Still, no one said anything.

"Did you see anything else in your grades that was suspicious?" one of the security guys asked. "Anything alarm bells ring for you?"

"Not really," Neecy said. "All my other grades were correct."

"How about you two?" Mrs. Hess asked. "This is the time to pass along anything that you think could help us with our investigation."

"There is something ..." Luther said slowly.

"Go ahead, son," the detective said. "What is it?"

"I got an e-mail a few nights ago that really spooked me. I didn't know what to do about it, so I didn't tell anyone."

"What kind of e-mail?" the detective asked.

"It was—this is really embarrassing," Luther said. "It was, you know, inappropriate. It had a picture attached. I don't know who sent it, but it seemed like maybe it was from a teacher here. I actually wondered ..." his voice trailed off.

"Go ahead," Mrs. Hess coaxed.

"I actually thought it might have been Mr. Sullivan who sent it," he said. "Especially after I saw that he had changed my grade."

"I never—" Mr. Sullivan started.

Mrs. Hess put a hand on his arm. "Mike, let this play out," she said. "Luther, was the e-mail from Mr. Sullivan?"

"I think it was," Luther said. "The name was 'TeacherCrusher.' And the message said something about how much he hoped I'd someday do what was in the picture."

"Wait, I got that e-mail too!" Chance said. "I didn't know who it was from, so I didn't bother to open the picture. I figured it was spam."

"How about you, Luther? Did you open the picture?" Mr. Fisher asked.

"Yeah. It was really disturbing," Luther said. "I deleted it right away. But it's probably still in my trash if you want to see it," he added helpfully.

"Sure, why not?" Mr. Fisher said. "Why don't you each sit at these laptops and log in so we can see these messages."

Luther and Chance walked around the table and logged in to their personal accounts.

"Here it is," Luther said.

Mr. Fisher read the e-mail. "Open the picture, please," he said.

Luther tried clicking. "I don't know what's

wrong," he said. "It opened at home. It was disgusting. It was like ... porn."

Neecy looked at Mr. Sullivan. He was slowly shaking his head back and forth.

Mr. Fisher clicked a few keys, and one of the security guys made a few suggestions. Then they all looked at the screen.

"What the—" Luther started. His expression went from fake innocence to what could only be described as absolute rage.

Mr. Fisher turned the computer around so that it was facing the rest of the group. On the screen was a picture of a Washington Redskins football player wearing jersey number twenty-one. Luther's face had been superimposed over the face of the real athlete.

"What was it about this photo that you found so disturbing?" Mr. Fisher asked. "You're dressed just like this today."

"But that's not the—" Luther stopped himself from saying anything more. He stood up and walked back to his seat. He threw himself down. Every muscle in his body seemed tense, like if he could, he would have punched the life out of someone.

"So this message says that the sender hoped someday you'd play for the Redskins. And you thought it was porn? How does this have anything to do with your math grade being changed? Help me out here, son, because none of this is making sense," Mr. Fisher said.

"We're ready over here too," one of the school system security guys said. "Same sender. Same message. Different picture."

He turned the computer around so everyone could see. On it was a group of graduates in caps and gowns. Chance's face had been superimposed over the face of one of the graduates.

Luther was breathing hard. Neecy wondered if everyone could hear how agitated he sounded.

"Sit back down, son," the man said to Chance.

Mr. Fisher pointed to something on the laptop he'd used to access Luther's e-mail. He clicked a few keys and stopped. Then the security guy clicked a few times on the laptop that held Chance's e-mail. Then he stopped.

"Boys, what are you playing at here?" Mr. Fisher asked. "Do you really think we're too stupid to know what you're up to?"

No one said a word.

"Why don't you tell us, Mr. Fisher?" Mrs. Hess said. She sounded puzzled.

"Well, these e-mails were forwarded to these students from other accounts. They didn't originate with TeacherCrusher, whoever that is. The original account names are at the bottom, so we can see where they were sent from initially."

"And?" Mrs. Hess urged.

"Are those your account names, gentlemen, 'HandsomeRansome' and ..." Mr. Fisher cleared his throat. "Um, 'TakeAChance'?"

"Get out!" Chance yelled. "I never—"

"Mrs. Hess," Mr. Fisher said incredulously. "They sent these e-mails to each other."

Luther shook his head slowly. Neecy would have bet he didn't know the e-mails had come from their accounts. Suddenly, she remembered the e-mail message from GoodTimeCharlieRay that resulted in her kissing Charlie. The same person *had* to be responsible.

"So let me get this straight," Mrs. Hess said. "Luther, you accused Mr. Sullivan of sending you an inappropriate e-mail with a disturbing photo attached. But the e-mail and photo was actually from Chance. And you sent Chance an e-mail and photo. Do I have that right?"

Luther said nothing. He just clenched and unclenched his hands.

"And as for you, Chance, you sent Luther an e-mail that—"

"*I did not!*" Chance yelled. "Look, I didn't know my grade was changed. I didn't pay any attention to that e-mail because I thought it was spam. And I never sent Luther any e-mail saying I hoped he'd play for the 'Skins. Someone's hacking, and it ain't me!"

"How about you, Luther?" Mrs. Hess asked. "Anything you want to say?"

"Yeah, find the hacker," he said. "Did you find my phone yet?"

"Your phone?" Mrs. Hess asked, confused. "What does your phone have to do with what we're discussing here?"

"Just asking," Luther said.

Neecy was confused by his question. It wasn't to the situation he was facing. She wondered what the connection could be between his phone and the changed grades.

"All right, we need to talk to decide how

we're going to proceed," Mrs. Hess said. "We don't have any proof that either of you accessed our grading system to change your own grades. Yet. But, Luther, you've made some very serious accusations about Mr. Sullivan. We *do* have proof that your accusations are lies. So you lied about a teacher. You and Chance sent each other the e-mails."

She turned to the school security guard. "Mr. Gable, please put Chance and Luther in separate offices for the time being, and then come back here. Neecy, you may go back to class. I hope we can count on you not to discuss this with anyone. And let me just say, we're all really proud of you for having done the right thing. I know when you talked to Mr. Sullivan about your grade, you had no idea how much you would help us uncover a real hacking scandal. So we are very grateful."

Neecy was warmed by the principal's words. She left the room and returned to class.

At lunchtime, JaQuel Rivas stopped by the table where Neecy and her friends were sitting.

"Bad news," he said. "I ran into Luther in the

hall. He was getting his stuff out of his locker. Both he and Chance are off the team."

The whole table expressed their shock.

"What'd they do?" Eva asked.

"Neither one of them made grades," JaQuel said.

"But they showed their report cards to Coach yesterday," Ferg said. "And they were fine."

"Apparently the wrong grades were posted."

"How is that even possible?" Joss said. "The whole system is computerized."

"I don't know, but that's what he said," JaQuel responded.

Neecy looked around the table. Each of her friends was looking at JaQuel as he talked.

Then someone caught her eye.

Keshawn Connor. He was at the next table.

And he was looking at her.

Their eyes held for a long moment, and then Keshawn raised an eyebrow and gave her a crooked smile.

Then Neecy knew.

She knew who sent the e-mails to Luther and Chance. She knew who raised her grade.

And she knew who had sent the e-mail that brought her and Charlie together.

She didn't know why, and she didn't know how. But she knew it was Keshawn.

"But here's the other thing," JaQuel said. "Chance is allowed to stay, but Luther's suspended for five days."

"No way!" Eva exclaimed. She turned to Neecy. "That should make you happy, Neecy," she joked. "A Luther-free week."

"Oh yes, the whole thing makes me very happy," Neecy said with a laugh. "In fact, I wish I could personally thank whoever was responsible. We'll probably never know, but he knows who he is and what he did. And he's my hero," she said.

"What makes you so sure it's a he?" Joss asked.

"Just a hunch," Neecy said. Then, when nobody was looking, she glanced at Keshawn and grinned.

CHAPTER 21

KESHAWN

Keshawn was impressed that Neecy figured it out. Or figured out some of it. When he heard her say he was her hero, he felt both good and bad. Sure, he fixed it, but she didn't realize that he had also created the mess in the first place. He hoped she never learned the whole story.

He would have given anything to know what had happened in Mrs. Hess's office. All he knew was that Neecy was called to the office, came back a while later, and rumors started flying about Luther and Chance being off the basketball team.

After school, Keshawn tried to go to the library, but there was a sign on the door saying it was closed for maintenance. He looked in and saw Mr. Fisher and a few other men in suits at the computers. Hopefully, they were uninstalling the keystroke-tracking program.

He started to walk toward the doors by the trophy case. The cheerleaders were practicing. Neecy was dressed for practice, but she had come out of the gym and was talking to Mr. Sullivan.

Keshawn pretended to be interested in the trophies while he strained to hear their conversation. The cheerleaders were so loud that he could only hear parts of it.

"Talked to the D.C. Stars … explained what happened and what you did … every teacher in this school … Whatever it takes to help you get your grades up to … asked me to tell you … Additional scholarship for good citizenship …"

So it seemed like Neecy might be all right after all. Keshawn left the building and began walking home. As soon as he got to the end of the parking lot where Bladensburg Road met Maryland Avenue, he saw Luther and Chance. They were waiting, and he knew they were waiting for him. He was in big trouble.

He stopped dead as they walked toward him. Luther pushed him in the chest so hard he fell. He stayed down. No sense getting pushed again.

"Think you're smart, moron?" Luther said. "You think this is gonna go away?"

"I don't think anything," Keshawn said. "I don't know what you're talking about."

Keshawn had been burned one other time for talking when he didn't know he was being recorded. He wasn't going to get burned again.

"Oh, now you're playing dumb too?" Luther said. "Well, guess what? That recording on my phone? I saved a copy of it on my computer at home. If you think this is over, you're even dumber than you look. It's not over till Luther Ransome says it's over."

Keshawn got up and dusted off the seat of his pants. "Actually, it's over when Keshawn Connor says it's over," he said. "That picture you gave me on the flash drive? The one you told me to bury in Mr. Sullivan's account? I didn't. I buried it in your account instead. It's on every computer you've touched since you gave it to me. You try anything, you touch me, you spread lies about me, then I tell the school and the cops where to look for it."

He was lying. Totally. But he hoped Luther didn't know that. Keshawn also hoped that the picture Luther had given him was inappropriate enough that the thought of it being on his computer accounts would keep Luther from ever messing with him again.

"You can't do that," Luther scoffed. "You can't access someone else's computer."

"Really?" Keshawn asked. "Well, NFL2B, you better hope you're right."

The look on Luther's face turned from anger to stunned horror. Keshawn knew Luther was realizing that access to Luther's password meant Keshawn had access to his accounts. Apparently it never dawned on Luther that if Keshawn could find a way into teachers' accounts, he could just as easily find a way into his.

The church ladies were right again, what goes around comes around.

"So this is it," Keshawn said. "It's over. We're even. I know what you did, and you know what I did. We're through. You ever try messing with me again, and I destroy you."

"You'll pay for this, Connor," Luther said as he turned to walk away.

"Oh, and one more thing," Keshawn called out.

The two thugs turned back to face him.

"I've left files everywhere that outline exactly what happened. Every threat. Every move. You ever touch me? There are people around town who know what to do. Anything ever happens to me? They open those files and take them straight to the cops. When I say we're done, we're done."

The look in Luther's eyes was murderous. He and Chance turned to walk away.

Keshawn reached into his pocket and turned off his cell phone so it wouldn't record any longer. Then he headed home.

As the church ladies would say, all's well that ends well.

Though that was actually Shakespeare.

ABOUT THE AUTHOR

Leslie McGill was raised in Pittsburgh. She attended Westminster College in New Wilmington, Pennsylvania, and American University in Washington, D.C. She lives in Silver Spring, Maryland, a suburb of Washington, D.C., where she works in a middle school library. She lives with her husband, a newspaper editor, and has two adult children, both of whom have chosen to live as far from home as possible.